HARRY THE HIGHRISE SPIDER

Elizabeth Downey

ISBN: 978-1-955245-17-3 (paperback)
ISBN: 978-1-955245-16-6 (hardcover)

First Edition Book, September 2021. Printed in the United States of America.

Book cover design, illustration, editing, and interior layout by:

www.1000storybooks.com

DEDICATION

To my two grandsons, Clark, age 8, and Reid, age 5, who assisted me in the writing of this book by offering their *brutally honest* evaluation of *Harry the Highrise Spider*.

Clark's input in particular highlighted and praised my extensive research on highrise spiders, declaring he had learned *a lot*!

Reid summarized his opinion of Harry rather succinctly (and with a major eye roll), by stating, "I hate to tell you, Nana, but dontcha know spiders don't talk?!"

Hi! I'm Harry, and I'm a spider. But I am no ordinary spider. I'm special.

I live on the twenty-fifth floor of a building in Chicago, because I love heights and I love being close to large bodies of water. But it's really all about the food. Being this close to Lake Michigan offers me an unlimited supply of insects, my favorite food! That's right, I'm not just here for the view; I'm here for the *bugs*!

My excellent ability to build webs is what keeps me fed because, lucky for me, my food flies straight into my web. Yum, a mosquito!

Honestly, I don't understand why humans don't like to eat bugs. If I were a human, I would choose bugs over a cheeseburger any day!

I'm sure you are wondering why I'm called "Harry the Highrise Spider." The spider specialists of the world actually call me a highrise flying spider, although I don't have any wings—and I'm delighted to tell you why!

When I was a baby spider, my mother taught me how to weave a special silk web so I could "fly."

"Harry," she told me, "you must build your web so it looks like a balloon. If you do that, the winds will take you high in the sky, and you can find a new home on one of these tall buildings. You will love living on a highrise building—the views are fantastic, and you'll never have to worry about running out of food! Besides, your brothers and sisters—Hector, Hillary, Hinckley, Heloise, Hugh, Humphrey, and all the others—have followed my advice and live the most wonderful life a highrise spider could ever dream of. Now it's your turn to fly high, Harry!"

So that's why I'm called a highrise flying spider—because I can use my web to float high into the sky!

Now, I may be a spider, but I am different from your typical "ground" variety. My body is round and black, so I can easily be seen from afar. And I can grow as large as the size of a half-dollar coin!

Unlike other spiders, I don't have eyelids on any of my eight eyes, which means my eyes never close. Instead, they remain open all day long, without blinking or closing.

But I still sleep. I sleep during the day, and I'm up at night, which means I'm nocturnal. And I have eight beautiful striped and spotted legs, which I think are my best feature. They really make me stand out!

Living way up at the top of my highrise building means I am always alone, and that is how I like it. My web is always full of tasty food and the weather up here is perfect: not too windy, not too rainy, not too cold.

But one morning, I woke up and saw another spider, on a nearby window, and that spider looked a lot like me!

I didn't like this one bit. I built my web way up here to be alone!

"Excuse me, sir," I shouted. "But this floor and window are taken! And I got here first! So please leave!"

"First of all," the other spider yelled back. "I'm not a sir, I'm a madam. And I didn't see a sign that said this window was taken, so just turn your many eyes in the other direction and you won't have to see me."

"Fine, but I'm not going to share my food with you!"

"No need," she replied. "I can catch my own. By the way, my name is Harriet. What's yours?"

"I'm Harry."

The following day, I woke up late in the afternoon and noticed that the sky looked darker than usual for this time of year. Then, just as I was about to enjoy my breakfast, a strong gust of wind almost knocked me off my web!

Immediately, I remembered what my mother taught me about dark skies and heavy wind: a Big Storm is coming!

I quickly anchored myself to my web with all eight legs. That's when I saw a bright flash of light, followed by a powerful *BOOM!* Out of nowhere, down came the rain in sheets and buckets!

I held on as best as I could, but I was scared. I didn't want to fly off my web! That's when I heard a faint voice call out: "Harry! Help! What's happening?"

That must be Harriet! I thought. *I can barely see her through the rain.*

"Harriet, it's a Big Storm! Just hold on to your web and swing with the wind. You'll be okay!"

"But Harry, I'm scared!" she cried. "This is my first storm."

"Mine too!" I yelled.

I had told her that we'd be okay, but soon I realized we may not be able to hold on for much longer. My legs were getting tired, and I was starting to feel sick from all the swinging.

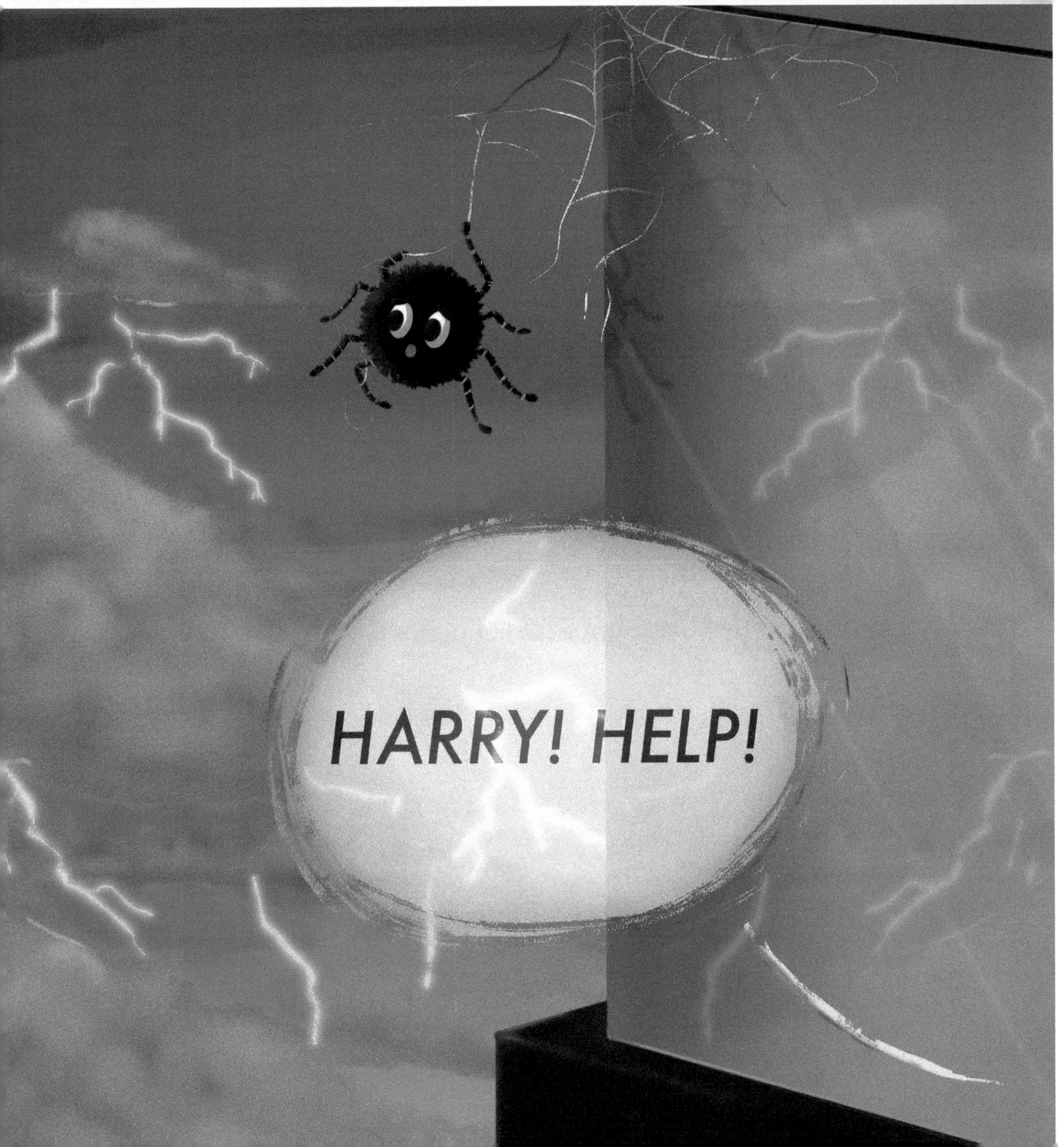
HARRY! HELP!

But before we knew it, the storm passed. The rain eased up and the wind died down to a warm summer breeze.

Harriet and I just survived our first storm together!

"Harriet, are you okay?" I called out.

"My legs feel a little shaky, but I think I'm fine," she answered.

With the storm finally gone, our troubles were over...

Or so we thought.

The next day, I looked up at the sky and saw a large board hanging above me. My curiosity quickly turned to fear when I heard the voices of two humans. Their voices were getting closer as the board descended.

Oh no, I thought. *Window washers!*

I had to get off my web and move to safety, but I also needed to warn Harriet! The humans were about to destroy both of our webs, and we needed to hide—or they might get us, too!

"Hide, Harriet!" I screamed. "The window washers are coming to clean us out!"

She didn't respond, but I was out of time. I climbed into my favorite hidey hole and settled in. I glanced out to see if she was still perched on her web, but there was no sign of Harriet. I hoped she found somewhere safe to go.

Moments later, the window washers were on our floor, and I could hear what they were saying:

"You know, Mortimer, people think that we window washers are afraid of heights. But not me. What terrifies me is the size of the spiders we find on these highrise buildings. They're huge!"

"I don't like 'em either, Ichabod," Mortimer replies. "The way they move creeps me out."

How rude! I thought. What makes these humans think that all of us are bad? We spiders are helpful and eat lots of bugs. We do a lot to make this city less buggy, and we deserve respect! I'll teach them a thing or two about spiders!

Window washing is often the most dangerous time for highrise spiders like me. It's a long day of waiting and hiding, which is very boring! But once they finish on my level, everything should be clear for me to rebuild my web. And I *need* to rebuild my web, because without a web, I have no food. And I'm getting hungry!

I looked over when the men were done washing the windows, and saw that Harriet had already started on her new web.

It made me feel good to see that she was safe. I like being alone, but it can be hard sometimes, which is why it's nice to have a friend nearby. And I have to admit, I like having Harriet as my next-window neighbor.

"You know, Harriet," I said as I began rebuilding my web. "It was nice having company through the Big Storm and the window washers. And I like talking with you."

"I feel the same way, Harry."

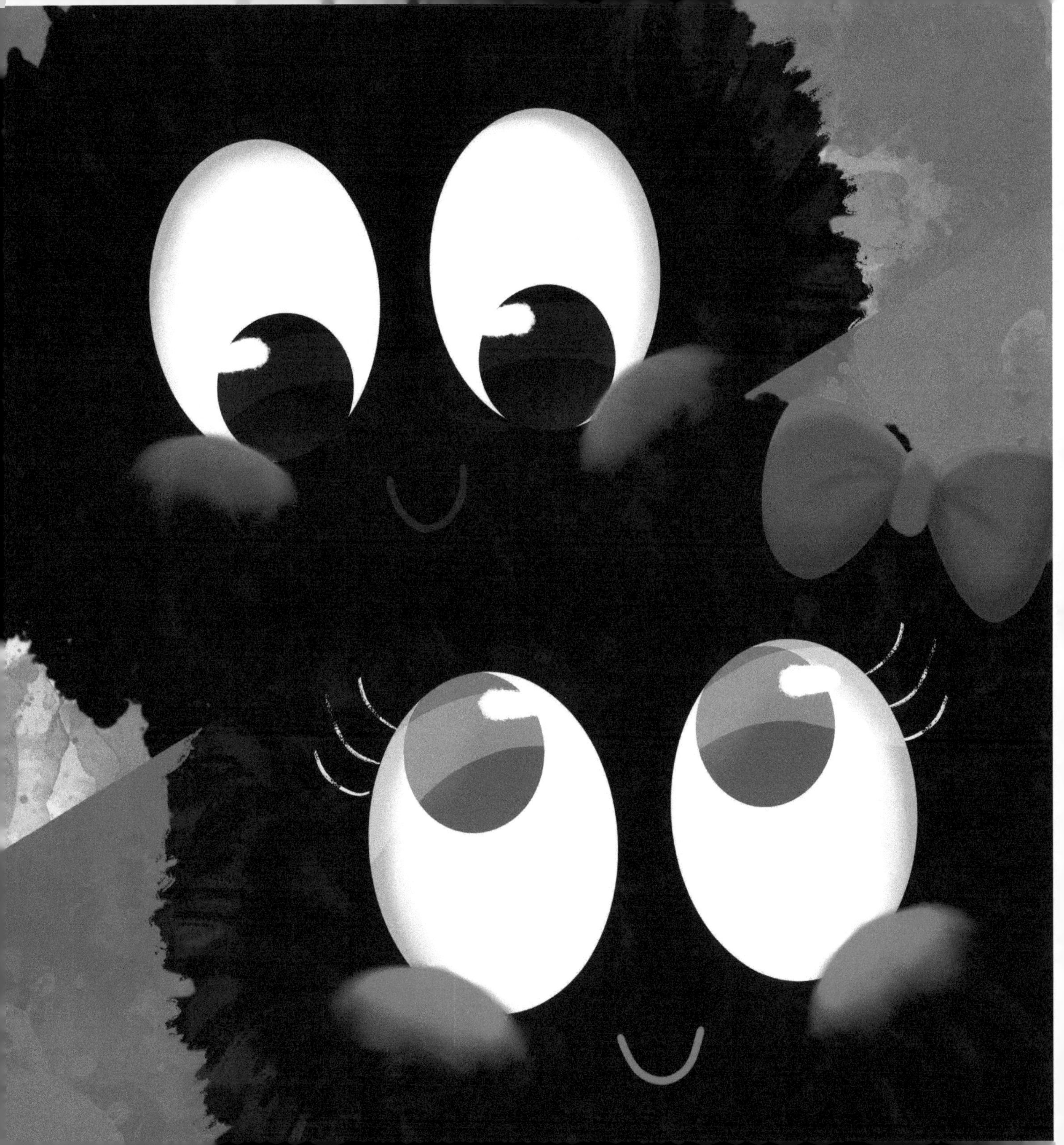

As the day went on, I found myself wanting Harriet to stick around—and perhaps even share a web with me. We both needed to rebuild our homes anyway, so it seemed like the perfect time to ask her.

"HEY HARRIET!" I shouted. "DO YOU WANNA SPEND YOUR LIFE WITH ME, SHARE MY WEB, AND HAVE HUNDREDS OF BABIES? YOU CAN EVEN EAT SOME OF MY GNATS!"

"Why on earth are you shouting at me?" Harriet asked.

"Sorry Harriet, I'm a bit nervous. What I mean to say is: I like having you around, and your webs are quite good. So I was wondering...do you want to build a web that we can live on together?"

"Why Harry, that sounds wonderful! I would love to share a web with you."

And that is exactly what we did!

ABOUT THE AUTHOR

Elizabeth Downey is a wife, a mother, a grandmother, and the author of *The Cat Who Came to Dinner: A True Rags-to-Riches Story.*

Having worked in the nonprofit sector since 1967, Liz is passionate about giving back to the community and the world around her. These days, she prefers to do this through writing and publishing feel-good essays about her unexpected encounters with animals.

Despite her severe allergies, Liz is a passionate observer of wildlife and an unwavering animal advocate, always finding innovative ways to protect any creature she crosses paths with. She also enjoys traveling and experiencing new things. In fact, she was able to get "up close and personal" with a mother lion and her cubs during a recent safari in Kenya.

As a Chicago-based author who enjoys interacting with her readers, Liz encourages those interested to get in touch by email at elizabeth.the.author@gmail.com.

CPSIA information can be obtained
at www.ICGtesting.com
Printed in the USA
BVHW021651120821
614282BV00007B/851

9 781955 245166